Shakespeare's
Greatest Stories
Abridged and Illustrated

W0082542

HAMLET

Wonder House

(An imprint of Prakash Books)

contact@wonderhousebooks.com

ISBN : 9789389432503

Cover image: Work of Pascal Dagnan-Bouveret, taken from https://commons.wikimedia.org/wiki/File:Pascal_Adolphe_Jean_Dagnan-Bouveret_-_Hamlet_and_the_Gravediggers.jpg

ABOUT THE AUTHOR
William Shakespeare

William Shakespeare is undoubtedly one of the greatest playwrights to have ever lived. He gained fame for his excellent ability to portray human emotions in the form of comedies, tragedies, tragic-comedies and historical plays. Some of his greatest plays include *Macbeth, Hamlet, Romeo and Juliet, The Merchant of Venice, A Midsummer Night's Dream, Julius Caesar, As You Like It, Othello, The Tempest*, and many more. He has been credited with giving the world a plethora of new words and phrases, which are used in our daily language today.

Popularly known as the "Bard of Avon", Shakespeare's contributions to literature are numerous and significant. Apart from plays, he also wrote sonnets and poems. Along with being a writer, Shakespeare was also a co-owner of a theatrical company named Lord Chamberlain's Men. Later, he became a co-owner of The Globe Theatre, which was built in 1599. The Globe is still one of the most cherished theatres in the world and manages to put up thrilling productions of Shakespeare's best works even today.

About the Author
William Shakespeare

William Shakespeare is undoubtedly one of the greatest playwrights to have ever lived. He gained fame for his excellent ability to portray human emotions in the form of comedies, tragedies, tragic-comedies and historical plays. Some of his greatest plays include *Macbeth, Hamlet, Romeo and Juliet, The Merchant of Venice, A Midsummer Night's Dream, Julius Caesar, As You Like It, Othello, The Tempest*, and many more. He has been credited with giving the world a plethora of new words and phrases, which are used in our daily language today.

Popularly known as the "Bard of Avon", Shakespeare's contributions to literature are numerous and significant. Apart from plays, he also wrote sonnets and poems. Along with being a writer, Shakespeare was also a co-owner of a theatrical company named Lord Chamberlain's Men. Later, he became a co-owner of The Globe Theatre, which was built in 1599. The Globe is still one of the most cherished theatres in the world and manages to put up thrilling productions of Shakespeare's best works even today.

Hamlet

Hamlet: The Prince of Denmark

Claudius: The King of Denmark and Hamlet's uncle

Gertrude: The Queen of Denmark, Hamlet's mother and wife of Claudius

Polonius: The Lord Chamberlain of Claudius's court

Ophelia: Polonius's daughter and Hamlet's lover

Laertes: Polonius's son

The Ghost: Ghost of Hamlet's dead father

Rosencrantz: Courtier and Hamlet's friend

Guildenstern: Courtier and Hamlet's friend

Marcellus: Guard and officer of the kingdom

Bernardo: Guard and officer of the kingdom

Francisco: A soldier and guardsman at Elsinore

" To be, or not to be: that is the question.

"

— **Hamlet**, ACT III, SCENE 2

Outside the palace of Wittenberg, a guard was intently surveying his surroundings for some movement. As the clock struck twelve, another guard came to replace him. It was too dark to recognise anyone, but the guards had to stay alert for the next forty-eight hours as instructed by the new king of Denmark, Claudius.

The new guard Bernardo said, "Francisco, you can go now. I am on guard tonight. And could you please ask

Horatio and Marcellus to come fast? They were ordered by the king to guard the palace with me."

Soon, Marcellus arrived. He cheerfully greeted, "Hello Bernardo. How are you doing today?" Bernardo gave him a strong handshake and asked, "Is Horatio coming?"

Marcellus rolled his eyes. "Horatio wouldn't believe that we saw something weird and scary last night. I thought it would be a good idea to bring him along tonight. Here he is!"

Horatio approached them, saying, "It was nothing, and I'm sure nothing is going to appear today as well." Bernardo smirked, "Horatio, sit here and wait for some time. You'll see it with your own eyes."

"Let's listen to Bernardo's story then," said Horatio.

Bernardo started, "Well, last night Marcellus and I were sitting here, staring at the star that is next to the north star. It had travelled across the night sky to the point where it is right now; we saw ..."

Suddenly, Marcellus said, "Everyone keep quiet! It's here." A ghost-like figure floated near them. Bernardo whispered, "Doesn't it look like the dead king?"

Marcellus whispered back, "Horatio, you're well-educated. What do you think it is?"

Horatio was stricken. "Well, he looks like the dead king ... but more terrifying!" He paused. Then said, "Dear ghost, whoever you are—why are you here? You look like our dead king and Hamlet's dear father. What is it that you want? I command you to speak."

The ghost suddenly disappeared in the fog. "Looks

like you offended the spirit. He's gone," said Marcellus. "He resembled the king," said Horatio. "The ghost was wearing the same armour as the king did when he fought the king of Norway."

"For the past two nights, the ghost has stalked us like a warrior," informed Marcellus. Horatio quietly said, "I don't know how to explain this, but this is a bad omen for us—for the palace and the people living here!"

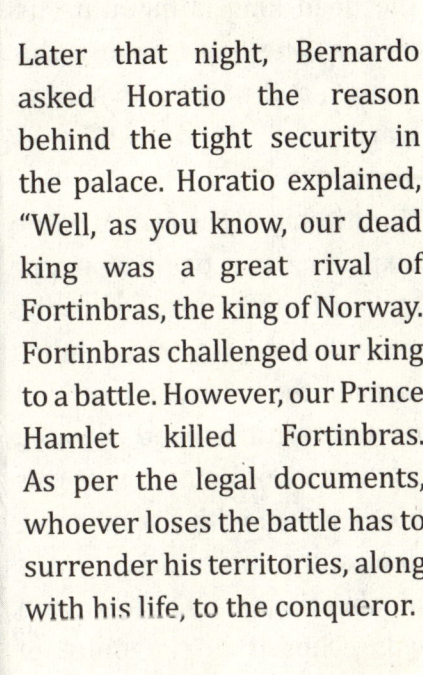

Later that night, Bernardo asked Horatio the reason behind the tight security in the palace. Horatio explained, "Well, as you know, our dead king was a great rival of Fortinbras, the king of Norway. Fortinbras challenged our king to a battle. However, our Prince Hamlet killed Fortinbras. As per the legal documents, whoever loses the battle has to surrender his territories, along with his life, to the conqueror.

So, Denmark now controls all their territories. However, Fortinbras' younger son, also called Fortinbras, demanded that our king return everything, which he refused to do. So now Fortinbras has gathered a bunch of thugs from the lawless outskirts of the country, who are willing to fight against Denmark. As far as I understand, that is the reason we are posted here tonight."

Bernardo replied, "I think that explains why the ghost of the dead king is haunting us. He was the one to cause this danger, and now he is here to warn us."

Horatio said, "The return of the dead king is a point of worry for our country. Just before the assassination of King Julius Caesar, the corpses rose out of their graves and flooded the streets of Rome; there was blood mixed with the morning dew, and unusual occurrences of shooting stars. The moon was eclipsed to the point of disappearing. Today after seeing the ghost here with my own two eyes, I feel this is a bad omen for us. It's like the earth and heaven have joined hands to warn us against the upcoming horrors."

Suddenly, the ghost appeared again. Horatio ordered Marcellus and Bernardo to stay where they were. Horatio called out, "You hallucination! If you are real, talk to me."

The ghost spread its arms as if it wanted to say something. A rooster crowed loudly nearby. Horatio commanded Marcellus to strike the ghost with a spear if it dared to move. Horatio shouted, "Over there, it is there!" However, the ghost had vanished into thin air again.

Marcellus said, "We were wrong to threaten the ghost, and anyway, we couldn't hurt the ghost. We were trying to hurt the air." Bernardo pointed out, "He was going to say something before the rooster created a racket."

Horatio said, "I have heard that roosters awaken the god of the day with their trumpet like crowing. It scares the ghosts away, just as we saw."

Marcellus nodded. "I have also heard that on the night of Christmas, roosters crow all night long, so that no ghost dares to wander around. The fairies' spells don't work and witches cannot bewitch us. That's how holy Christmas night is!"

Horatio concluded the conversation by saying, "I think we should inform Hamlet about this encounter with the ghost of his father. What do you say?" Marcellus agreed.

The next morning, Polonius, the Lord Chamberlain of Claudius's court, his younger daughter Ophelia, elder son Laertes, and Gertrude, Hamlet's mother, eagerly waited for Claudius to take over responsibility as the king of Denmark.

As Claudius entered the court and strode towards the throne, he said, "My dear friends and family, I, Claudius, have to take over the throne of Denmark due to my brother's sudden death. He was a genuine and pure soul."

His mirth masked by his kind words, he continued, "I know I should be mourning for my brother, but due to Fortinbras and his regular attacks on Denmark, I have decided to step up and fulfil my responsibilities."

He looked at Gertrude with utter affection, but to hide his true feelings from the court, he said, "I have married my brother's wife as advised by you all. Hence, please accept me as the new king of Denmark."

> **"I have married my brother's wife as advised by you all. Hence, please accept me as the new king of Denmark."**

Claudius finished his speech and took possession of the throne grandly.

Claudius announced, "Now back to business. As you all know, our enemy Fortinbras is revolting against us, underestimating my power and strength to rule a country. He keeps pestering me with demands like giving him his land back, which his father lost to my elder brother."

Claudius revealed that he planned to send a letter to Fortinbras' uncle, the current king, who was unaware of his nephew's plans. Claudius addressed Laertes, "I heard you wanted to talk to me. What is it that you need?"

Laertes replied, "My lord, as you know, I left my work in France for your coronation. Now I think it's time for me to resume my duty there, if you agree!" Claudius immediately accepted his request and permitted him to leave.

Soon, Prince Hamlet entered the court. Claudius greeted him, "My dear Hamlet, how are you? I haven't met you since your father's death."

"Too many family ties! I wish I could run away," Hamlet thought. Queen Gertrude said, "My dear Hamlet, please stop wearing these gloomy black clothes and be friendly with your uncle. You cannot spend your entire life mourning your father. What lives must die, and then become eternal. It happens all the time."

Hamlet avoided her eyes. "Yes mother, it happens all the time."

"Then why do you seem so very grim?"

Hamlet raised his eyes defiantly. "Seem? I don't know what you think of these black clothes, my weeping, sad face or my downcast eyes, mother, but let me tell you— they are just a hint of what I feel. There is a storm of grief inside my heart, which cannot be explained or felt just by talking about it."

Claudius interrupted him, "My dear Hamlet! You are a pure soul, but you need to understand that as you are mourning for your father, your father must have mourned for his father, and he for his father. Someday, every son has to mourn his father. But spending most of your life in desolation is not going to do you any good. So please stop thinking about your father. I will try to be a father to you."

Claudius waited for an answer, but it never came. Disheartened, he continued, "Hamlet, I love you as much as your father did. I know you plan on going back to Wittenberg. However, your mother and I want you to stay here, and be one of the ministers in the court. You'll be a guiding light for me."

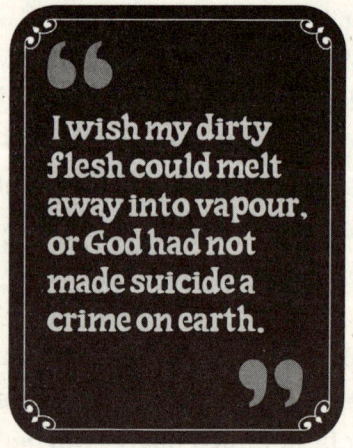

> I wish my dirty flesh could melt away into vapour, or God had not made suicide a crime on earth.

"Hamlet, please listen to him. Stay here. Don't go back to Wittenberg. I need you, my son!" Gertrude implored him.

Hamlet replied, "I respect you mother, and I am ready to follow your orders."

"This is the answer I was expecting! Now, as my dear son has agreed to stay in Denmark, I feel we should celebrate!" Claudius exclaimed.

Hamlet quietly lamented, "What an unfortunate day! My father was such a loving person. And now I have lost my mother too. She married my uncle as soon as my father died. Even before the tears had dried from her cheeks, she had fallen in love again."

Hamlet wept in a corner, "Oh God, please take my life. I wish my dirty flesh could melt away into vapour, or God had not made suicide a crime on earth. I wish I could kill myself. God, please listen to me, kill me or give me a reason to live."

That evening, Horatio, Marcellus and Bernardo visited Hamlet in his chamber. Hamlet was surprised to see them all together. "What are you all doing here? Is something wrong at Wittenberg?"

Horatio replied, "I thought of skipping school today, sir!"

"I wouldn't even allow my enemies to do that," Hamlet smiled. "But I am sure that is not the reason you've travelled all the way from Wittenberg to Elsinore, is it?

"Sir, we wanted to attend your father's funeral," said Horatio.

Hamlet turned fidgety at the mention of his father. "Please don't mock me. I know you're here to attend my mother's wedding."

Horatio squeezed Hamlet's shoulder. "Sir, I am very sorry for your loss. I saw your father once in Wittenberg. He was an admirable king and an amazing father." Hamlet brushed away a stray tear with his bare hand and said, "Yes, and what breaks me more is that I'll never be able to see him again."

Horatio hesitated. "Sir, I think I saw your father yesterday." Hamlet stopped short and glared at Horatio. "What are you talking about? This is no time to joke around!" Horatio and Marcellus narrated the entire incident to Hamlet.

"But where did this happen?" Hamlet asked after a few moments of dead silence.

Marcellus replied, "Sir, we saw him near the platform where we stand guard at night." Horatio told Hamlet about the rooster as well.

Hamlet cocked his brow. "That is strange. Are you both guarding tonight as well? I'll accompany you and speak to the ghost. I don't care whether the heavens try to stop me or hell tortures me; I will confront it. Also, don't tell anyone else about this. Let it be a secret between us. I want to handle this myself. Thank you for informing me."

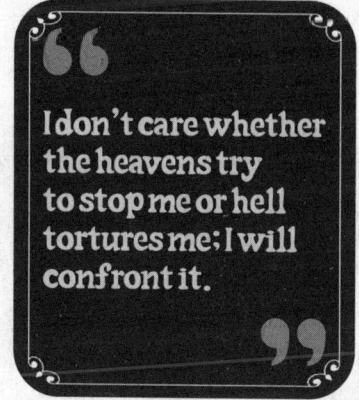

I don't care whether the heavens try to stop me or hell tortures me; I will confront it.

As they left, Hamlet sat by the window and pondered, "My father, all armed and angry. Something is very wrong. I wish the night were here. I can't wait to meet him. Now all the unrevealed truths will be out in the open. But, till then, I have to be calm and patient."

Meanwhile, Laertes was making preparations to leave the country when Ophelia entered his chamber.

"I have packed everything, and the bags are loaded on the ship. Now, my little sister, I want you to write to me every day. I will be far, but not so far that I can't reach you on time! Yes?" He smiled at her affectionately.

Ophelia assured him, "Brother, do you think I won't write to you?"

Laertes reasoned, "Ophelia, I know that you love Hamlet, and he loves you, but it won't be wrong to say that with great power comes great responsibility." She frowned.

"Hamlet is a servant to his family's obligations," said Laertes. "He belongs to a royal family, and they expect him to be part of the court, fulfil his duties and take care of the country. So don't be upset if he chooses his country over you. Please understand, it's his priority and it will always be!"

Ophelia replied, "Brother, I'll keep your words of wisdom close to my heart. You'll never regret my decisions. I promise you!"

Soon, Polonius arrived and wished Laertes good luck for his journey. He said, "Son, always remember a few rules of life. Don't believe everyone. Make friends and be truthful to them, but not too much. Once you have tested your friends and their reliability, hold on to them. Also, don't pick a fight without reason, but if you find yourself in one, stand up for yourself. Listen to people, but talk to few. Last but not the least, never borrow money." Laertes bid goodbye to his family and left Denmark by sea.

Meanwhile, Hamlet was standing with Bernardo, Horatio, and Marcellus outside the gates of Wittenberg palace. "The air is biting cold, isn't it?" he said. "Yes, it's definitely nippy," Horatio replied. Hamlet rubbed his hands together. "So when does the ghost appear exactly?"

Marcellus replied, "Right about now. I am sure it's going to greet us in a few minutes." While Horatio and Hamlet were talking about the state of things, Marcellus shouted, "Sir, look, here it is!"

Hamlet turned around and stood still, petrified, wondering what to do next. He took a step forward and said, "I don't know who you are, but please be an aid to sort out my confusion." While Hamlet was staring at the spirit, it hastily moved towards him. Hamlet got scared and hid his face in his hands.

In a few moments, Hamlet composed himself and said, "Oh dear spirit, please help us. Tell us who you are."

The ghost remained motionless. "Don't drive me crazy with curiosity. Please tell me who you are. You look like my father! Why have your church-buried bones burst out of the coffin? Why are you wandering on earth?"

The ghost gestured Hamlet to follow him. Horatio said, "Hamlet, the spirit wants you to follow it. I suppose it has some secrets to share!"

Marcellus pointed out, "Look how politely it's standing there, waiting for you. Don't go!"

"But it won't speak until I follow it," said Hamlet.

"No sir, don't!"

"Why not? I don't care about my life anymore. It's calling me, I have to go."

Horatio grabbed Hamlet's hand. "No sir, what if it tempts you to jump into a well or the deep blue sea?"

Horatio and Marcellus refused to let him go.

Hamlet insisted, "Let go of me!" He drew his sword and said, "I swear if you don't let me go, I'll make a ghost out of you both." They released him immediately. Hamlet walked ahead and they decided to follow him.

After a cold, long walk, Hamlet stopped. "Look, I am not following you any farther. You have to reveal the secret now!"

The ghost croaked, "Hamlet, I am the ghost of your father, doomed to walk the earth for a long time ... I can only wander around at night, in the day I burn in the flames of purgatory."

"What?" exclaimed Hamlet, alarmed.

The spirit said, "If you ever loved me, please take revenge for my murder!"

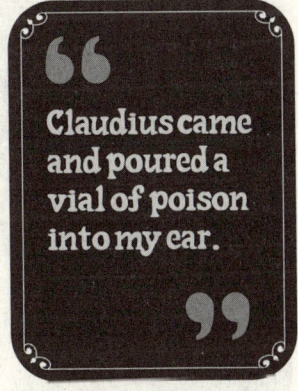

"Claudius came and poured a vial of poison into my ear."

"Murder! No, my father died due to a snake bite."

"No, my son. Everyone was told that I was bitten by a poisonous snake. Denmark was fooled. The truth is the real snake that stung me is now wearing my crown."

Hamlet was aghast. "I knew it! My uncle!"

The spirit said, "My son, I was sleeping that afternoon, in the orchard, like I always did. Claudius came and poured a vial of poison into my ear. This poison quickly spreads in your veins and curdles your blood, which is exactly what happened to me. And that's how my brother robbed me of my life, my crown and my queen. Your uncle slayed me in the midst of a sinful life."

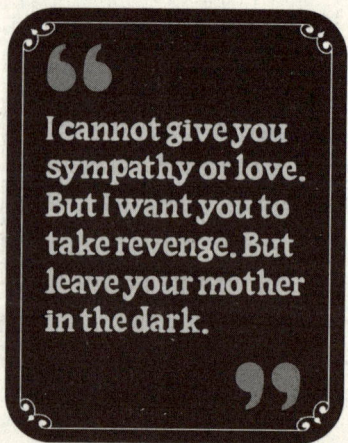

> I cannot give you sympathy or love. But I want you to take revenge. But leave your mother in the dark.

Hamlet wept helplessly as the ghost of his father recounted his murder. "My son, I cannot give you love or sympathy. But I want you to take revenge. But leave your mother in the dark. Let God punish her. I bid you goodbye. Remember me. I love you, my dear Hamlet."

While Hamlet mourned for his father, Marcellus and Horatio caught up to him. Reluctantly, Hamlet told them the truth. He made them swear they wouldn't reveal the truth until his father had been avenged. Soon, Hamlet left for Denmark.

One afternoon, a couple of days later, Ophelia came running to Polonius. "Father, Hamlet has gone mad!"

Polonius tried to calm her down and asked, "Ophelia, what happened? What did he do?"

"Father, Hamlet came into my chamber. He was drunk and dirty. His clothes were torn and he couldn't even walk properly. He grabbed me and held me close to him."

She took a deep breath, "Hamlet looked at me like an artist stares at his art. And then he just left. I don't know what to do." Polonius asked Ophelia to accompany him to the king.

"Father, please wait! I did something that might have hurt him. I did what you told me to do. I returned all of his letters and gifts. I asked him to never visit me again!"

"That is why he has gone crazy." Polonius sighed heavily.

"Now I regret my decision. I should have judged his love before giving you any advice. I am very sorry, my child. I thought he was just toying around with you. It's the universal nature of old people to think that we know more

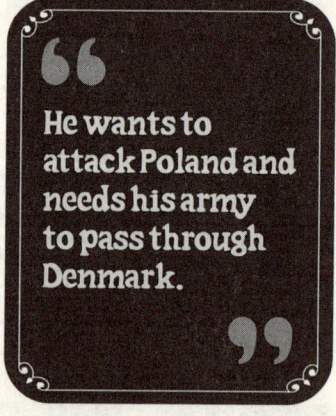

than the younger generation. Never mind, we have to go to the king and narrate the entire incident."

Meanwhile, Claudius was having a meeting with Hamlet's close friends, Guildenstern and Rosencrantz.

He said, "Gentlemen, I have called you here today to talk about your friend. As you know, recently, Hamlet had gone through much emotional trauma. You've been friends since you were children and you know him inside-out. So, I want you both to stay and spend some time with him. Find out what's troubling him. I need your help to get him back on track."

Rosencrantz said, "My lord, it is our duty to obey your command, and it will be fulfilled, we assure you."

Claudius smiled warmly. "Great, then I request you to pay him a visit right away. Servants, please take these gentlemen to Hamlet's chamber." Claudius and Gertrude were left alone in the court.

Soon, Ambassador Voltemand entered and said, "My king, as you commanded, I met the king of Norway and he has assured our safety. However, he has requested something from you." Claudius' eyebrows shot up.

The ambassador continued, "He wants to attack Poland and needs his army to pass through Denmark. These are the documents."

Claudius agreed immediately and asked the servant to send an official acceptance letter to the king.

After a while, Polonius came to the court with a stack of letters and reported everything that Hamlet had done. Gertrude and Claudius became worried, discussed Hamlet's behaviour and asked Polonius what he thought of Hamlet.

Polonius confessed that he'd thought Hamlet was just playing around with his daughter and so he'd asked her to stay away from him. Claudius interrupted him, "So, this is why Hamlet is behaving this way!" Polonius nodded and gave them all the letters Hamlet had sent Ophelia.

Gertrude read the letters over and over again. "Is he going insane with love? And if he is, then how do we find out?"

Polonius said, "My lady, I have a plan. The next time he's here, I will send my daughter to meet him. We can watch

them from behind the curtains and judge his behaviour. If he doesn't react the way I'm predicting, then you can relief me from my duties immediately." Gertrude and Claudius agreed to the plan.

Later that evening, Hamlet was wandering around the palace grounds when he bumped into Rosencrantz and Guildenstern. He was surprised to see his old friends together.

"Rosencrantz and Guildenstern, how are you? How come you're here?"

Rosencrantz replied, "We're good, friend. We just wanted to meet you. It's been long."

"You know Rosencrantz, nowadays, people don't interest me!" said Hamlet.

"Well sir, if people don't interest you, then I think the actors we met today won't interest you either?" Guildenstern added, "A drama company of tragic actors have arrived from the city. You used to enjoy their performances, back in the day."

33

A servant interrupted them to announce the arrival of the theatre company. Hamlet requested him to send them up. As the actors arrived, Hamlet welcomed them with a handshake and a smile on his face. One of the actors said, "My lord, I don't know if you recognise us, but we definitely remember you!"

"I distinctly remember you," said Hamlet. "Your drama company does the best tragedy, comedy, pastoral, history, tragical-history, one-act, tragic-comical-history plays, and long poems, right?" The actors were taken aback.

Polonius entered the chamber and Hamlet ordered him to take care of the actors and escort them to their rooms. When Hamlet was the only one left behind, he secretively called one of the actors. "Sir, can you enact *The Murder of Gonzago*?" he asked. The actor nodded. Hamlet requested him to recite a few extra lines written by him for the play and bid him adieu.

Hamlet mused, "Murder has no tongue, but it always finds a way to speak the truth. I will make the actors enact the scene of my father's death. I'll observe Claudius's expressions during the play. I'll probe his conscience. If he flinches and becomes pale, I'll know he is the culprit. I can't simply trust the ghost. It can be a devil disguised as my dead father.

"I need stronger evidence than the ghost to work upon. This play will be an aid in revealing the truth, and then I'll know what to do," he continued.

Later that evening, Rosencrantz and Guildenstern met Claudius, Gertrude, Polonius and Ophelia. Claudius enquired after Hamlet's unusual behaviour. Rosencrantz informed them that Hamlet had admitted to feeling strange but he didn't know why; he had seemed a little different and was dancing around their questions, never giving them straight answers.

Guildenstern added that Hamlet seemed to have forced himself to be friendly with them. Gertrude asked them if they'd tried to tempt Hamlet with some entertainment.

"Yes, my lady, we informed him of the arrival of the theatre troupe. He seems quite interested, and has asked them to put on a performance tonight. They agreed and are here at the court right now." Polonius added, "My Queen, he has also requested that you and King Claudius attend the play."

Claudius said, "I am delighted to hear that! Gentlemen, I urge you to encourage his interest even more."

Once the two men left, Claudius requested Gertrude to leave the room as well, as they were about to spy on Hamlet while he talked to Ophelia. Before leaving, Gertrude said, "Ophelia, I hope Hamlet is behaving unreasonably only because of your love. I really want to see the two of you married; I believe you will turn him into a sane man again."

Ophelia smiled, "Me too, madam."

Polonius and Claudius hid behind the curtains as Hamlet walked into the hall. Ophelia greeted him. Hamlet gazed at her.

"Good evening, my lady."

Ophelia replied, "My lord, I haven't seen you for days. How are you doing?"

"I am well, Ophelia. Thank you."

"My lord, I have a few mementos of yours lying with me. I meant to return them to you."

"Mementos? Ophelia, I haven't given you anything."

"Don't do this Hamlet ... You sent me letters with those mementos, which made the gifts so much more precious. But they've lost all meaning now. So I request you to take them back."

Hamlet had a strange look in his eyes. "My lady, I know you are beautiful, but that doesn't mean you are a good person. The power of beauty can turn a good woman. You are rotten at the very core. I used to love you, but not anymore."

"You misled me then!" shouted Ophelia, and thus began a long argument.

Hamlet accused Ophelia of being a scammer while she accused him of insanity.

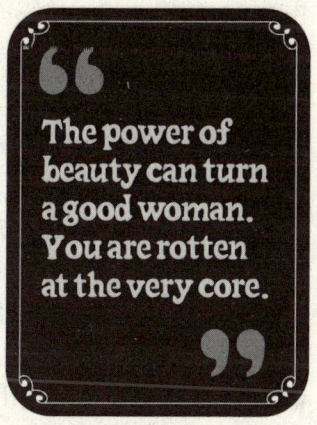

The power of beauty can turn a good woman. You are rotten at the very core.

Finally, Hamlet stormed out, leaving Ophelia alone and broken. She whispered, "God, please bring my Hamlet back. He was such a loving person. Hamlet had a gentleman's grace, a soldier's strength and a scholar's wit. He used to be the pride of the country. I don't know what happened to him, I don't know him anymore ..." Weeping, she ran out of the hall.

Claudius and Polonius came out of their hiding. They couldn't believe their ears. The scene they'd witnessed was baffling. Claudius was now sure that Hamlet's unusual behaviour had nothing to do with Ophelia; something else was bothering him.

Later that day, Hamlet met the same actor he'd spoken to earlier. "I hope you're ready!" he said. The actor nodded. He added, "Listen, please don't exaggerate your emotions on stage. I hate actors who get swept away by passion.

But don't look too tame either. Fit the action to the word and the word to the action." The actor nodded again and left to rehearse. Hamlet met Polonius and requested him to get the king and queen ready for the play.

As Hamlet was preparing for the performance, Horatio grabbed his shoulder. Hamlet greeted him with a firm handshake and said, "Horatio, you are my best friend. I am sure you know that. Today evening, while the performers are enacting my father's death scene, I want you to observe the reactions on my uncle's face. If he flinches, I'll know that he is the murderer. However, if it doesn't affect him, then the ghost is just a devil playing with my emotions."

Soon Claudius, Gertrude, Guildenstern, Rosencrantz, Polonius and Ophelia assembled in the hall and took their designated seats. Hamlet decided to sit with Ophelia.

As everyone settled down, the actors started coming in. The play began with a king and queen sitting near a waterfall. They embraced each other lovingly and lay down on a bank of flowers. The king gradually fell into a deep sleep. The queen noticed him sleeping peacefully.

She kissed his forehead and left.

Suddenly, a man came in, took the king's crown and poured poison into his ear. When the queen returned with a basket full of flowers, she found the king dead. She went hysterical.

A while later, the murderer returned with three other people from the palace and began consoling the queen. His aim was to get close to her. At first, she was cold to him, but gradually, she started reciprocating his love.

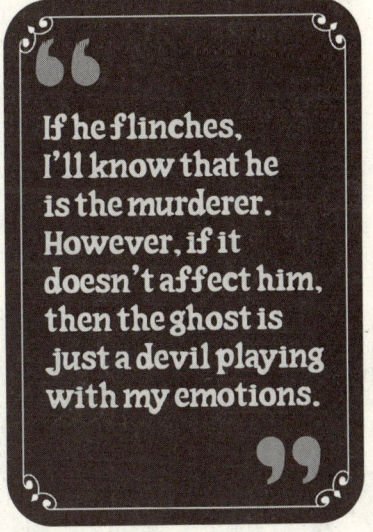

> If he flinches, I'll know that he is the murderer. However, if it doesn't affect him, then the ghost is just a devil playing with my emotions.

"What play is this?" asked Claudius.

"It is called *The Mousetrap*. It's about a person called Gonzago, who is a duke, and his wife Baptista. Gonzago was murdered in Vienna.

Please watch the entire play and give me your reviews. It's one of my favourites," said Hamlet.

As the play moved forward, Claudius got more and more restless. Horatio was staring at the king as the nephew killed his own uncle during the course of the play. "The ghost was right. It was the wrathful spirit of the dead king. I don't know how Hamlet will react to this," thought Horatio.

Hamlet said loudly, "You see how he poisoned the king

in his own garden? The murderer is Gonzago's nephew. You'll soon see how the nephew gains the queen's love as well."

Suddenly, Claudius stood up and said, "Turn on the lights. Get me out of here. Stop the show!" Gertrude, worried, asked him if he was feeling fine. Claudius left the hall in a hurry, and everyone else dispersed.

Hamlet approached Horatio. "Horatio, did you notice Claudius? I am sure the ghost was right. Did you notice his expression when the actor was pouring poison in the king's ear?"

"Yes, I watched him very closely," replied Horatio. Hamlet was thrilled. He asked the musicians to play a musical rhythm. Rosencrantz and Guildenstern walked in on Hamlet in his musical reverie.

"Sir, can I have a word with you?" said Guildenstern.

Hamlet replied, "Sure, Guildenstern. You can have a story with me, why just a word?"

Guildenstern said sternly, "Sir, the king ..."

Hamlet interjected, "What about the king?"

"Sir, the king is in his chamber and is extremely upset."

"My dear friend, you should inform a doctor then, not me. If I treat him, he'll only get more frustrated."

"Sir, please stick to the point. It's important."

Hamlet stood up straight. "Yes, I'll try my best not to fool around. Please speak."

Guildenstern sighed, thoroughly fed up. "Sir, the queen has sent me here to tell you that she and the king are really upset with you. She says that your behaviour has astonished her."

"Oh, what a wonderful son I am!" Hamlet exclaimed.

Rosencrantz said, "Sir, she wants to talk to you. Alone." Hamlet left like an obedient child.

Soon after, Claudius met Guildenstern and Rosencrantz in his chamber. Claudius yelled, "That's it! I cannot let his insanity grow out of control. I don't like the way Hamlet is behaving. You both prepare yourselves, I am sending you to England on business, and I want you to take Hamlet with you. I cannot risk the danger he poses as he grows crazier by the hour."

Guildenstern assured him, "My lord, please don't worry. We'll take care of him."

Rosencrantz said, "Everyone tries to stay away from harm, but a public figure demands even more protection. When a leader dies, he doesn't die alone. Like a cyclone,

the king takes everything down with him. We cannot risk him hurting you, my lord!" Accepting Claudius' orders, they left to make preparations for England.

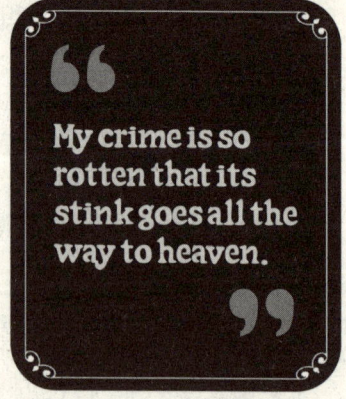

> My crime is so rotten that its stink goes all the way to heaven.

Before Claudius could rest Polonius walked in. "My lord, Hamlet is going to visit his mother in her chamber. I wish to monitor their conversation. I am here to ask for permission."

Claudius said, "Polonius, you are my friend. You can do as you please, just don't get caught."

"Don't worry. I'll take special care. I'll visit you before going to bed. Thank you, sir."

Now alone, Claudius thought, "My crime is so rotten that its stink goes all the way to heaven. My hand has an invisible mark of Cain on it ... I have killed my brother."

For a brief moment Claudius felt guilty, but the next moment he pitied himself.

"So what if I have the curse of Cain and my hands are coated with my brother's blood? Doesn't heaven have enough rain to wash it away? Isn't that why God has mercy in His heart for His children? Am I not His dear child?"

Claudius' eyes turned to the sky. "I pray to you every day for two things only—to keep me away from sinning and forgive me for my sins. God, you have to help me. Keep me from committing sins and forgive me for the ones I've already committed. Please forgive me for this horrible murder."

Claudius got up and plucked the crown from his head. "I guess my prayers will go unanswered because I am still reaping the rewards of my sin. Is it possible to gain forgiveness and still enjoy the fruit of the crime?"

Meanwhile, Hamlet was entering Claudius's chamber. He saw Claudius on his knees asking for forgiveness. "This is the right time. I should kill him now," he thought quietly. Hamlet drew his sword and moved towards his uncle.

💀

He stopped suddenly. "What am I doing? I can't kill him while he's praying. He will go straight to heaven. He murdered my father when he was enjoying a life of sin. My father must be in hell, and so should Claudius. I will get him when he's indulging in his own sins." Hamlet put his sword back in its sheath and walked towards his mother's chamber.

Polonius announced Hamlet's arrival to Gertrude.

"Madam, you have to be blunt with him. Tell him that his stupid prank could have caused real trouble. Remind him that King Claudius has already faced the consequences of his actions. I will be here, but I won't say a word," said Polonius. Right then, Hamlet shouted from outside the chamber, "Mother! Mother! Are you there?" Polonius hid behind the curtains just as Hamlet pushed the door open.

Hamlet slowly walked towards Gertrude. "Mother, now what is this all about?"

"Hamlet, you insulted your father," she snapped.

"No, mother. You insulted my father!"

"Son, your answers are foolish!"

"Mother, your questions are evil."

"Hamlet, have you forgotten who I am?" Gertrude cried.

Hamlet mocked her, "No, not at all! I know that you're the queen. You are the wife of your husband's brother and, of course, you are my mother, which I deeply regret."

Gertrude was furious. "Well, in that case, I will call someone whose existence you don't regret."

"Oh no, mother, you are not going anywhere till I hold up a mirror to show you what you are."

"So what are you going to do, kill me? You know you won't." With that, she screamed for help.

Polonius instinctively screamed, "Help! Help! Help!" from behind the curtains. Hamlet turned and stabbed Polonius through the curtain.

Gertrude cried, "What have you done, Hamlet!"

"Why, was it your dear husband and my new king?"

"What a senseless, horrible act."

Hamlet replied, "Senseless, horrible act! More than killing your husband and marrying his brother, my sweet mother?" Gertrude was aghast, "Killing my husband?"

Hamlet stepped back and pulled the curtains to reveal Polonius, bloody and dead. He didn't flinch as he let go of the curtains. "Oh, I thought it was somebody more worthy of dying. Well, you deserved it anyway, you nosy fool!"

Gertrude fell to her knees and wept, "What have I done to you, my child? Why are you being so cruel?"

Hamlet pulled his mother by the arm and said, "See this picture over here, mother. Two brothers are standing together. Look at this one, my father. He was such a genuine soul. A soul who couldn't hurt anybody, couldn't cheat his brother, who wouldn't consider any other woman above you; and what did you do? Betrayed him, played with his emotions, killed him and married his younger brother. How could you, mother? How could you? I feel sick."

Gertrude begged Hamlet to let her go. "Hamlet, you make me hate myself. Your words are like daggers in my heart. They are killing me."

The ghost suddenly materialised and said, "Hamlet, stop it! You're scaring your mother. Leave her alone. I told you to talk to her, not torture her. You're no one to punish her. She will reap what she has sown. For now, just speak to her."

As the ghost disappeared, Hamlet let go of his mother's arm. "Hamlet, are you fine?" Gertrude gasped. "You're staring at the air, talking to nobody and you're on edge. Please calm down. Ease your mind."

Hamlet politely informed Gertrude that he was leaving for England that day with Guildenstern and Rosencrantz. He bid her goodnight and dragged away Polonius' body.

Claudius burst into Gertrude's chamber and found her frozen. "Gertrude, where is Hamlet?"

"Claudius, you won't believe what I witnessed today!" Gertrude exclaimed.

Claudius held her gently. "What is it?" Shakily, Gertrude told him everything that had happened.

"Oh my God! This is terrible. That could have been me had I been standing in Polonius's place." He took a deep breath and continued carefully, "Gertrude, Hamlet is

a threat to everyone. If I don't contain him, people will blame me for his heinous crimes. I love Hamlet from the bottom of my heart. But I have kept his condition a secret from the entire kingdom, and now he is becoming a serious threat to everyone. I have to stop him. Where is he?"

"He has gone to dispose the corpse. A part of him still has a conscience though; he wept for his heinous crime."

Claudius replied, "We'll send him to England soon. I'll use all my political connections to exempt Hamlet from his crime."

Claudius asked Guildenstern and Rosencrantz to find Hamlet and bring the corpse back to the chapel. He wanted to bury Polonius in the chapel and conduct all the rituals properly. Hamlet, far away from the castle, had already hidden Polonius's body. Guildenstern and Rosencrantz found Hamlet wandering around aimlessly a few hours later.

"Prince, stop! Please tell us, where is Polonius's body?"

Hamlet shrugged, "I have hidden it safely."

They persisted, but Hamlet refused to reveal where the body was hidden. Tired of questioning him, Rosencrantz and Guildenstern left him alone.

Meanwhile, Claudius was anxiously pacing in the courtroom. He was preoccupied with only one thought.

"It is so dangerous to leave a madman on the loose. He will destroy everything. My plan will fail if he comes back to the palace. I want to capture him but I can't, the public loves him.

They love him so much that they will not understand the severity of his crime. They will judge me for keeping my brother's son in prison. I think we should appear calm and just. Sending him away should look like a carefully considered move. But a terminal disease cannot be cured by temporary medicines. It has to be cured with extreme treatment … or be removed for good."

I killed my brother…

Now I will kill my brother's son.

Soon, Rosencrantz entered the courtroom. Claudius strode towards his throne, asking, "So, Rosencrantz, where is the body?"

Rosencrantz replied, "My lord, we were unable to get him to reveal where he has hid the body."

"Fine. Where is Hamlet then?"

"Sir, he is waiting for your orders to come in." Claudius signalled for him to be let in.

He narrowed his eyes, "Hamlet, where is the body of my dear friend?"

Hamlet replied, "At dinner!"

"At dinner?"

"Yes! The difference is that he isn't eating, rather he is being eaten. By worms and maggots."

Furious, Claudius shot up from his throne. "Hamlet, where is the body?" he demanded. Hamlet gave a crooked smile and said, "Well! I think you should ask your messengers to check in heaven. If they don't find him there, you can always check in hell yourself. However, if you don't find him within a month or so, you'll definitely smell him in the main hall." Claudius instructed his servants to look for Polonius's body along the main hall.

"Father, you don't need to hurry. He is not going anywhere!" Hamlet chuckled.

Claudius replied warily, "Hamlet, I care for you as much as I cry for my dear friend Polonius. I want to give you another chance. The ship is ready, the wind is favourable, and your bags are packed—I want you to go to England."

Hamlet tilted his head in confusion, "England?"

"Yes, England."

"Good, then I am off to England."

As Hamlet walked out, Claudius asked his attendants to follow him to make sure he boarded the ship as soon as possible. Everyone departed except for Claudius. He sat on the throne and wrote a letter to the king of England. It read, "Dear Sir, I am sure you're still suffering from the damage caused to you by Denmark. So, out of fear and respect, I am sure you won't deny or ignore my request—kill Hamlet!

I need you to do so immediately. Until and unless you complete that task, I cannot rest. Thus, I request you to kill Hamlet as soon as possible."

Meanwhile, Hamlet had reached the port and met the captain of a troop. He stopped the captain and asked, "Sir, where is your army headed?"

The captain replied, "Sir, this troop is going towards Poland to capture some of their land."

"And whose troops are these?"

"The Norwegian king's, led by Fortinbras," replied the captain. Hamlet thanked him for the information and asked Rosencrantz and Guildenstern to move ahead without him.

"What am I doing?" he thought. "Rather than taking revenge for my father's murder, I am going to England. What is the meaning of a life that simply aspires to eat, sleep and dream? I've the motive and I've the willingness to take revenge. So why have I not done it yet? I will kill Claudius and fulfil my destiny! From now on, if my thoughts are not violent, I'll consider them worthless!"

Back in Denmark, Horatio knocked on Gertrude's chamber. "I am not in the mood to meet anyone right now," she called out.

"My lady, Ophelia is out of her mind. She keeps talking about her father and the conspiracies against him. She is beating herself up and weeping constantly. I request you to see her at once."

Gertrude asked Horatio to let her in. Ophelia strolled in singing,

He's dead and gone, lady,
He's dead and gone,
At his head, a grass-green turf,
At his heels a stone!

Gertrude was horrified. "What are you doing Ophelia? What does this song even mean? What happened to you, my dear? Oh, Ophelia!"

Ophelia interrupted Gertrude, "Please listen, my lady. White his shroud as mountain snow..." Suddenly Claudius walked in and saw Ophelia singing madly. "My God, look at this poor girl. Is she talking about her father?" Gertrude nodded her head uncertainly. Ophelia piped up, "Let's not talk about that. Listen to this,

Tomorrow is Saint Valentine's day,
All in the morning betime,
And I a maid at your window,
To be your Valentine.
Then up he rose, and donned his clothes,
And dupped the chamber door.
Let in the maid that out a maid
Never departed more."

Claudius turned to Gertrude, "How long has she been like this?"

Before he could get a reply, Ophelia's wretched voice cut through her song. "I can't bear the thought of him lying dead in the cold ground. My brother will hear about this. Thank you, lord and lady. I take your leave now!"

Claudius directed Horatio to follow Ophelia and take care of her.

"My dear Gertrude, she has lost her father, there are nasty rumours about his death, and now Hamlet has gone to England. When bad news knocks on the door, it doesn't knock one at a time, but all at once, like an army. Ophelia has been robbed of her senses, without which we are all just animals. And now, Laertes is back from France as well. He's getting swayed by rumours surrounding his father's death. I am sure he'll blame me for this."

Suddenly, Gertrude and Claudius heard some voices outside the palace gates.

Gertrude said, "Messenger, please check what's happening."

The messenger rushed back to the chamber. "My lord, there is a group of people standing outside screaming that Laertes should be the king of Denmark. It's like an ocean of people, wanting to bring a storm of change in the constitution. Please hide, my lord!"

The doors to the chamber smashed open and Laertes entered the room with his army. He ordered them to wait outside. Laertes pointed accusingly at Claudius. "You vile king, give me my father back!"

Gertrude reached out to Laertes and said, "Laertes, stop. Please calm down!"

"My lady, I have only one drop of calm blood in me and even that is telling me to avenge my father's murder."

Claudius cried, "Gertrude, please let him go. Let him come to me."

Laertes demanded, "Where is my father, you ruthless king?"

"He's dead."

Gertrude hastily interjected, "But the King didn't kill him."

Laertes cried out in anger, "Don't toy with me! Forget my allegiance to you! I don't care if I'm damned. I have vowed to take revenge for my father's death, and I will!"

Claudius said, "Laertes, please give me a chance to prove that I am innocent. I know who is responsible for your father's death."

Suddenly, Ophelia waltzed in singing a gloomy song. It pained Laertes to see his sister acting like a madwoman.

And will he not come again?
And will he not come again?
No, no, he is dead,
Go to thy deathbed.
He never will come again
his beard was as white as snow
All flaxen was his poll.
He is gone, he is gone,
And we cast away moan,
God ha' mercy on his soul-
And of all christian souls,
i pray God. God be wi' ye

Ophelia waltzed out and Laertes' eyes followed her with immense grief. Claudius addressed Laertes, "Son, I request you to choose a friend of yours and tell him the entire incident. If he finds me guilty for your father's murder, I'll give up my crown, my kingdom, and my life. However, if he finds me innocent, I will help you capture the culprit and get revenge."

Somewhere in the palace a servant approached Horatio, followed by a few sailors. "Sir, I have a letter for you from Prince Hamlet." The letter read,

Dear Horatio,

Please take these men to see the king. They have letters for him. We weren't even at sea for two days when a pirate ship attacked us. We were too slow to escape, so we had to fight. They took me as a prisoner on their ship. They have treated me quite kindly, but want me to grant them a favour.

Once you give the letters to the king, the sailors will bring you to me. I have a lot to tell you, especially about Guildenstern and Rosencrantz. Please be quick!

Your trusted friend,
Hamlet

Meanwhile, Claudius exposed Hamlet as Polonius' murderer. Laertes confronted him for not arresting Hamlet. Claudius replied, "My friend, there are two reasons for my decision. First, the queen, his mother, is devoted to him. I cannot lose her at any cost. The second reason is that the public loves him. I find them dismissing all his faults, no matter what. Thus, I need someone to punish Hamlet without my interference."

A messenger entered and said, "Sir, these are letters from Prince Hamlet for you and the queen." Claudius took the letters and asked Laertes to stay and hear them. The letter said, "High and mighty one, I have to return to Denmark, suddenly. I will come and tell you my reason behind returning so soon."

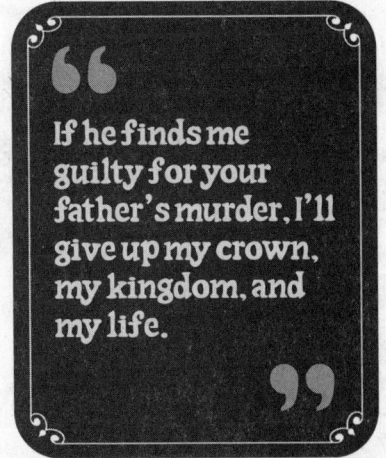

If he finds me guilty for your father's murder, I'll give up my crown, my kingdom, and my life.

Claudius and Laertes were shocked, but Laertes said, "Let him return, my lord. At least I'll have a chance to look him in the eyes and accuse him of killing my father."

Claudius replied, "Laertes, I hope you'll let me help you!" Laertes agreed.

Claudius confessed, "I have a few plans in mind to kill him. In fact, no one will blame us for the murder, even his mother will call it an accident. Laertes, you stay in your room. As Hamlet enters the palace, I'll boast about your ability to win wars and woo women. As far as I know Hamlet, he will get jealous. In short, we get you both to fight and place bets on you. Hamlet, being an overconfident, righteous and gullible fellow, will not notice the difference between the swords, so you can easily pick up the sword with the sharpest edge, and in one thrust you can kill him."

Laertes replied grimly, "I will dip the sword in poison, so

he dies instantly."

"But, my friend, if the first plan fails, we need another plan to rely upon. I'll keep a drink spiked with poison near me. When Hamlet feels tired, I'll offer him the drink," said Claudius.

As Claudius and Laertes joined hands, Gertrude entered the chamber. "My lord, you were right. Bad news doesn't come one at a time, it comes in an army," she cried.

Claudius took Gertrude's hand and said, "Gertrude, my dear, what happened?"

Gertrude choked, "Laertes, you sister Ophelia drowned. She is no more."

Laertes cried, "Drowned!"

Before Gertrude and Claudius could say anything, Laertes stormed out. Claudius said, "Gertrude, let's follow him. I tried so hard to calm him down. Now he'll be more eager than ever to take revenge. We have to restrain him."

The next day, Hamlet and Horatio met by a graveyard. They saw a gravedigger singing while digging a grave. Hamlet was disturbed by his indifference. He said, "Horatio, doesn't this man feel for the corpse lying right next to him? He is singing!"

Horatio replied, "My friend, he is so used to this job that it doesn't matter to him anymore." However, Hamlet couldn't bear to see the gravedigger playing around with the skulls of people who were once alive.

He shouted from afar, "Sir, I hope you don't mind me asking—whose grave is this?"

The digger replied, "It's mine, sir." A quick smile escaped Hamlet. He walked towards the graveyard.

"I meant, what man are you digging the grave for?"

"Sir, this is not for a man or a woman! It's for someone who used to be a woman, who just passed away." Suddenly they

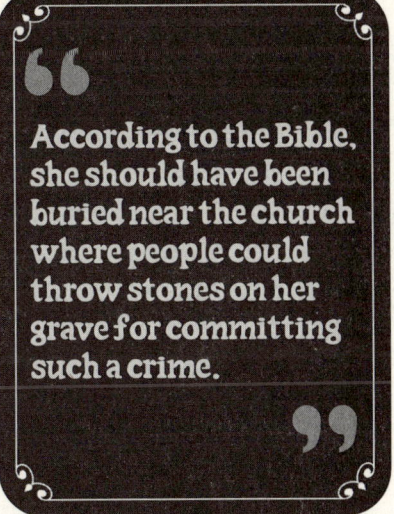

> According to the Bible, she should have been buried near the church where people could throw stones on her grave for committing such a crime.

noticed Queen Gertrude, King Claudius, Laertes and the high priest walking towards the graveyard with a coffin. Hamlet motioned for Horatio to hide.

Laertes asked the priest, "What other rites are left?"

The priest replied, "Laertes, although she was a pure soul, she committed suicide. Thus, it is impossible to fulfil all the rites. According to the *Bible*, she should have been buried near the church where people could throw stones on her grave for committing such a crime. However, she was loved by everyone. So the king asked us to bring her here to complete her last rituals."

💀

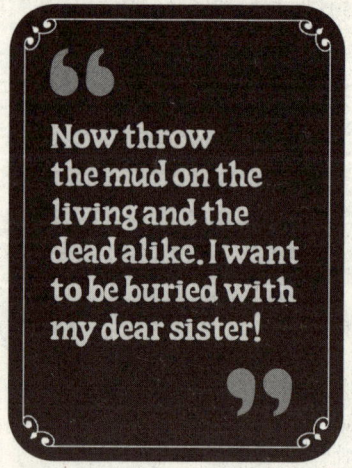

> Now throw the mud on the living and the dead alike. I want to be buried with my dear sister!

Laertes was furious. "Priest, you will burn in hell for saying this! While my dear sister enjoys her time in heaven!"

Hamlet was shocked. With pain stinging his eyes and trembling lips, he said, "What, my dear Ophelia?" While Hamlet was crying over Ophelia's death, everyone was giving their last blessings to her. Queen Gertrude showered her body with flowers and said, "My sweet girl, I once thought that you would be my Hamlet's wife, and I would shower these flowers on your wedding day. This is not what I desired. Rest in peace, Ophelia."

Suddenly, Laertes jumped into her grave and clutched her tight in his arms. He cried, "Now throw the mud on the living and the dead alike. I want to be buried with my dear sister!"

Seeing Laertes, Hamlet also jumped into the grave. Laertes was astonished to see him. He threw a punch at Hamlet and they wrestled each other. Claudius commanded the servants to pull them apart.

Horatio shouted, "My lord, please control yourself. It's a grave, not a wrestling ground!"

The servants pulled them apart. As Hamlet and Laertes shook them off, Hamlet said, "I can fight with him over this my entire life."

"Over what?" asked Gertrude.

Hamlet replied, "I loved Ophelia. Laertes and his father separated us. They poisoned her mind against me. Let me

tell you, my friend, even if forty thousand brothers claim their love for Ophelia—no one, and I mean no one, can match the amount of love I have for her."

"Oh, don't listen to him Laertes. He's crazy!" said Claudius. Hamlet cried, "What do you think, you are the only one who loves Ophelia? Show me what you can do for her. Will you stop eating? Will you cry? Drink vinegar? Eat a crocodile? I'd do it for her. Would you? What were you trying to prove by jumping in that grave?"

Gertrude grabbed Hamlet's hand. "This is insanity! Please, everyone calm down. Hamlet is going to be like this for a while. Eventually, he'll come to his senses. I request you all to be patient." Hamlet pushed her hand and walked away. Claudius ordered Horatio to follow him.

Claudius whispered to Laertes, "Laertes, my son, please remember the talk we had last night. Be patient. We will find a solution soon."

Laertes nodded and sombrely completed Ophelia's last rites. Meanwhile, Hamlet and Horatio reached the palace. Hamlet informed Horatio that Guildenstern and Rosencrantz were killed by English soldiers.

"King Claudius had set a trap for me. Horatio, do you still want me to remain calm? Don't you think I must kill this man? He killed my father, stole my mother from me, took the throne that I'd hoped for, and tried to get me killed!"

A messenger knocked on the door and said, "My lord, I am here to inform you that King Claudius has placed a large bet on you against Laertes, son of Sir Polonius." Hamlet gestured the messenger to leave the room. "Horatio, I don't want to fight. I am going for a walk. In case they still want me to fight, I have my sword." Hamlet was leaving the room when a servant bumped into him.

"I apologise, my lord." Hamlet ignored him but the servant continued, "My lord, the king and queen want you to fight Laertes. They are calling you to the hall for a duel."

Everyone gathered in the hall decorated with trumpets, drums, fencing swords, tables and pitchers of wine. Claudius asked Hamlet and Laertes to shake hands before the duel. Hamlet said, "My dear friend, I apologise for insulting you today in the graveyard. Everyone knows that I am suffering from a mental illness. Thus, it is not my mistake, I am a victim; my illness is to be blamed."

Laertes said icily, "Although my feelings are satisfied, my honour isn't. I cannot forget what you did to my father and sister. Nothing can stop me from taking my revenge."

He stepped towards Hamlet. "I can't forgive you so fast. If I make peace with you, my reputation will be tarnished. I accept your love as love, but I can't do anything about it."

Hamlet asked the attendants to pass the swords. Claudius said, "Before the fight commences, we know that Laertes is a trained fighter. Therefore, we have given him a handicap. He'll only have three hits to win."

He instructed a servant to put the goblets of wine on a nearby table.

"If Hamlet makes the first or second hit, or comes back with the third hit, I'll drink to Hamlet's health. I'll also drop a pearl in the goblet for Hamlet. The pearl is costlier than all the pearls in the crowns of the last four Danish kings. Now, I want the soldiers to salute Hamlet whenever he makes a move against Laertes."

Hamlet and Laertes began fencing. Hamlet screamed, "This was a hit!"

Laertes replied, "No, it wasn't." Hamlet called for the referee.

The referee said, "It was a hit."

"Fine. Let's continue," said Laertes.

Claudius dropped a pearl in the goblet and roared, "This is for my son!" Hamlet and Laertes fenced again.

Hamlet screamed, "It was again a hit!"

Laertes replied, "You got me, it was."

Gertrude said, "My son is out of breath. Hamlet, here take my handkerchief. Wipe your sweat, son." Gertrude picked up the goblet of wine and said, "I'll drink to my son, his victory, health and happiness." Claudius watched, horrified, and screamed, "Gertrude, don't!"

Before he could stop her, Gertrude took a sip. It was the poisoned drink; but now it was too late for Gertrude.

But Hamlet was only focused on the duel. "Laertes, you are treating me like a child. Strike harder, my friend!"

Laertes replied, "I don't think so. Come on. Let's fight!"

Hamlet and Laertes fenced again but this time, the strike was harder. Laertes wounded Hamlet with his sword, and in a rush of actions, Hamlet grabbed Laertes' sword and hit him with it.

Suddenly, Laertes collapsed and Gertrude fell from her throne. Claudius hastily said, "I think she fainted at the sight of them fighting."

Gertrude cried, "No, Hamlet. The drink! The drink was poisoned!" And she stopped breathing. Laertes confessed that the sword had been dipped in poison and died on the spot. Hamlet ran towards Claudius and forced him to gulp down the poisonous drink. He left Claudius to die in his suffering.

The poison in his body had spread by now. Hamlet collapsed and called for Horatio, "Horatio, I am dying. I don't have time, I want you to tell everyone the real story behind this revenge."

Horatio's eyes welled up. "My dear friend, I can't live without you. I'll also drink from this goblet and follow you to heaven."

Hamlet snatched the goblet from him. He requested Horatio to postpone his dream of sweet relief from the cruel world, and tell the true story of greed, sacrifice, pain, revenge, and death, to others. Hamlet slowly closed his eyes and fell into the arms of death.

Soon, Fortinbras entered with his army and was greeted by the bloodbath. "I came here to claim the kingdom, but I believe the kingdom is already mine. Horatio, please tell me what happened here." Horatio narrated the story.

Fortinbras said, "Soldiers, pick up Hamlet's body with respect. Fire your guns in honour of Hamlet, the true king of Denmark."

He stepped out of the palace to speak to the people of Denmark. "Your prince Hamlet was a great soul. He would have been a great king, if he only had a chance to prove himself. A sight like this suits the battlefield, but here at the court, it shows how much went wrong. Denmark will always remember the pain and sacrifice of Prince Hamlet. May God bless his soul. For Prince Hamlet."

The guns fired, and everyone bowed their heads in silence.

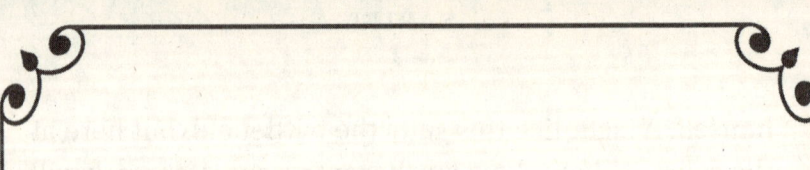
I must be cruel only to be kind;
Thus bad begins, and worse remains behind.

– **Hamlet**, Act III, Scene 4

Hamlet

Hamlet is a play by William Shakespeare published between 1600-1601, and first performed in 1602. *Hamlet* is considered to be Shakespeare's most complicated revenge tragedy of all time. Regardless of the time, year and society, Shakespeare, through *Hamlet*, challenged the genre of tragedy and questioned the nature of revenge itself.

The play revolves around the themes of death, love, revenge, uncertainty, decay and corruption, action vs. inaction, sanity vs. insanity, and appearance vs. reality. It shows the devastating death of a faithful son, revengeful nephew and a beloved lover.

Hamlet encompasses a few characteristic features of a tragic story, namely a vengeful spirit, a hero driven to madness, and a play within a play. Shakespeare also used symbolic elements to portray love and hatred such as skulls, graveyards, and goblets full of poison.

Themes

REVENGE

Revenge dramas were the favourite form of tragedies in the Elizabethan and Jacobean eras, which found its highest level of expression in *Hamlet*.

'Revenge' as a theme was introduced in the Jacobean era only for the purpose of entertainment. Shakespeare continued to use it as a theme in many of his plays, namely *Hamlet, The Merchant of Venice, Macbeth* and more. However, after extensive analysis and studies, 'revenge' became a way of exploring several human emotions and behaviours, hence, making the plays much more serious and intricate.

Hamlet's source of madness and his revenge seeking spirit is partly derived from society and its code of conduct. Every society has a code of conduct and rules on how to behave and act in different circumstances. There are many instances in the story where one person directs another on how to behave. For example, Polonius lectures Laertes on the practical rules of life, Polonius and Laertes convince Ophelia to keep her distance from Hamlet, Hamlet constantly struggles to make peace between his "duty" as a faithful son and his emotions as an individual. In *Hamlet*, the codes of conduct are primarily dominated by religion and aristocracy, one that demands revenge in exchange for the degradation of one's honour.

MADNESS

Hamlet overplays his mental struggle to get a confession out of the murderer of his father. However, as Hamlet begins to crave revenge, he discovers that the codes of conduct don't make it easy to gain vengeance against another human being. But his refusal to avenge his father would make him an unlawful son. Hamlet's act of madness, and his struggle with the idea of revenge eventually lead him into a descent to real madness, one that he doesn't recognise himself. The line between the act and the reality get so blurred that Hamlet ends up becoming the man that he only intended as a pretence.

Answer me!

Q1. At the beginning of the story, why was Elsinore under strict security?

Q2. Do you think love is an important theme in the story? Explain.

Q3. Explain the relationship between Hamlet and his mother, Gertrude.

Q4. We do not know much about Claudius and his past. Imagine Claudius as a young man based on what you know and write his story in not more than 500 words.

Q5. Write a character sketch of the protagonist.

Q6. Were the steps taken by Hamlet to avenge his father's death justifiable? Discuss.

Q7. Do you think Hamlet's behaviour towards Ophelia was too harsh? Explain with examples.

Q8. Do you sympathise with Hamlet as a character? Why?

Q9. Do you think the ghost was real or a figment of Hamlet's imagination? Explain.

Q10. Explain the play that takes place within Hamlet.

Q11. Is death one of the major themes of the story? Explain with examples.

Q12. Explain the role Rosencrantz and Guildenstern play in Hamlet's life.

Q13. Do you think Hamlet's indecisiveness was the reason behind his behaviour and untimely death?

Q14. What is the difference between Hamlet and

Ophelia's madness? Explain.

Q15. Based on Hamlet's extreme reaction to his father's death, do you think Hamlet would make a great king? Give reasons for your answer.

Q16. Do you think you empathised with any of the characters in the story? If yes, who was it and why?

Q17. Despise and revenge are the two essential themes of this play. Explain with examples.

Q18. If you were to rewrite the story of *Hamlet*, what would you change?

Q19. At the end of the story, Fortinbras asks the countrymen to pay their respects to Hamlet as a soldier and a son, and the true king of Denmark. Do you agree?

Q20. Do you think Hamlet is a tragic hero?

Q21. Introduce a new character in *Hamlet* who would change the plot line.

Q22. Hamlet's conspiracy to kill Claudius leads to the death of many others. Do you think Hamlet was solely responsible for his own tragedy? Could there have been a happy ending to the story?

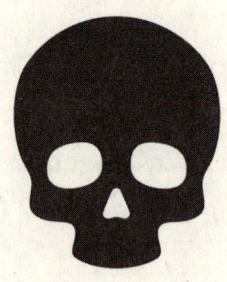

The end.